D1529352

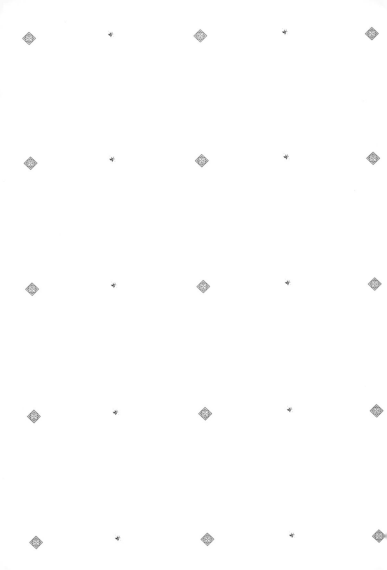

Jack and the Beanstalk

Louis Weber, C.E.O.
Publications International, Ltd.
7373 North Cicero Avenue
Lincolnwood, Illinois 60646

Manufactured in China.

8 7 6 5 4 3 2 1

ISBN: 0-7853-2607-3

Publications International, Ltd.

Jack and the Beanstalk

Cover illustrated by
Deborah Colvin Borgo

Illustrated by
Susan Spellman

Adapted by
Sarah Toast

Publications International, Ltd.

*T*here was once a poor widow who lived with her son, Jack, far out in the country. Jack was good-natured but lazy. When at last there was no money left to buy food, Jack's mother told him to take the dairy cow to market and sell her for a good price.

On his way to market, Jack met a strange man who asked him where he was going with the cow.

"I'm going to market to sell her," he said.

"I will give you these five magic beans for the cow," said the strange man.

Jack thought that was a good bargain, so he traded one cow for five beans.

Jack hurried home and said, "Look at the five beans I got for the cow!"

"You foolish, lazy boy!" cried his mother angrily. "Now we will go hungry." She threw all the beans out the window, and she and Jack went to bed without any supper.

When Jack awoke early the next morning, he noticed an odd shadow across his window. He ran outside to see that a huge beanstalk had sprung up during the night. It grew so high he could not see the top.

Jack was curious and decided to climb up the beanstalk. He climbed for hours. When he finally reached the top, he saw a great castle in the clouds.

The magnificent castle, set there on the highest cloudy hill, looked as if it were a vision in a dream. Jack knew from his tired arms and legs that he had not just dreamed his long climb, but he rubbed his eyes to make sure he wasn't seeing things.

From this far away, the castle looked larger and finer than any Jack had ever seen. He stepped carefully off the beanstalk and walked slowly to the castle.

As he got closer, Jack realized that the castle was too large for anyone of his size. "This castle must belong to a giant!" Jack thought to himself.

Continuing the long walk to the castle, Jack met a beautiful fairy. She told Jack that the giant who lived in the castle had killed Jack's father long ago and had stolen all his gold. The tiny fairy said that he should take back what was rightfully his, and then she disappeared.

When Jack reached the steps, he asked the giant's huge wife for some supper.

"If you stay here, the giant will have you for supper," she said. But Jack was so hungry that he begged to eat there anyway.

The woman gave in and fixed Jack a good supper. He had just finished eating when he heard the thump, thump of heavy footsteps.

Just as the giant entered the kitchen, his wife hid Jack in the oven. The giant sniffed the air and roared, "Fee-fi-fo-fum! I smell the blood of an Englishman!"

"It's just your supper," said his wife.

The giant ate his enormous supper in one huge swallow. Then he said, "Fetch my gold."

The woman brought bags of gold coins that had belonged to Jack's father. The giant fell fast asleep counting the money.

Jack crept out of the oven, took a bag of gold, and ran back to the beanstalk. He threw the bag down to his mother's garden and climbed down as fast as he could.

Jack's mother was overcome with joy when gold coins rained down and Jack came down after. They could now take care of their needs for awhile. But then one day the gold ran out.

Jack decided to disguise himself and climb up the beanstalk again. He wanted to get back more of his father's gold.

When Jack returned to the castle, tired and hungry, the giant's wife did not want to help him.

"The last hungry boy I helped stole a bag of my husband's gold," she said. But Jack was so polite that she finally let him in and gave him a drink of water.

Just then the giant's huge footsteps shook the floor. Jack barely had time to hide in the oven before the giant entered the kitchen and roared angrily, "Fee-fi-fo-fum, I smell the blood of an Englishman!"

"Don't be silly," said the giant's wife as she put supper on the table. The giant ate his supper greedily, and then he told his wife to bring him his hen.

Jack heard the giant shout, "Lay!" When he peeked through a hole in the oven, he saw the hen lay a perfect golden egg. After he told the hen to lay three golden eggs, the giant fell asleep. Jack leaped out of the oven, snatched the hen, and ran.

When Jack reached the beanstalk, he began to climb down quickly. He took the wonderful hen to his mother. The hen laid a golden egg every time it was commanded to. With the golden eggs, Jack and his mother were able to fix up the cottage, and there was always plenty to eat.

After a while, however, Jack thought about what the fairy said to him about his father. He decided to climb back up the beanstalk. When he reached the top, Jack sneaked back into the castle and hid in a pot.

When the giant thumped into the kitchen, he sniffed the air. "Fee-fi-fo-fum!" His wife was startled. She scurried over to the oven and looked in, but it was empty.

The giant's huge wife looked around the kitchen, but she didn't find Jack. After the giant ate his supper, he called for his magic harp. His wife brought his beautiful harp of purest gold.

When the mean giant commanded the harp to play, its golden strings began to play, and it made the most entrancing music Jack had ever heard. Not only that, the harp even sang in a high, sweet voice.

It wasn't long before the giant was lulled to sleep by the music. When Jack heard the giant snoring, he knew it was safe to climb out of the pot. He grabbed the giant's harp and started to run off with it.

"Master! Master!" the harp cried. The giant awoke with a start. Jack jumped off the table, the harp in his arms, just as the giant made a grab for him. Jack held tightly onto the harp and ran for his life.

Jack could hear the huge thump, thump of the giant's footsteps closing in behind him. He knew the giant took large steps, so his fear was great. But the giant had just finished a filling supper, and that slowed him down enough for Jack to reach the beanstalk ahead of the giant.

Jack climbed down the beanstalk clumsily with the harp, calling out to his mother as he went. "Mother! Bring me the axe!"

The giant was halfway down the beanstalk when Jack reached the ground. Jack took the axe from his mother. With one mighty chop, he cut the beanstalk in two. The giant crashed to the ground and died.

Jack, his mother, the hen, and the harp lived happily ever after.

The

End

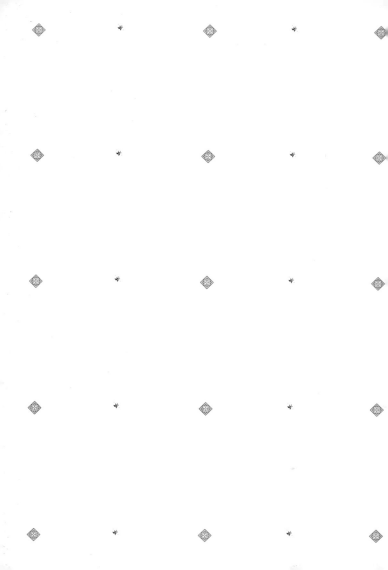